A Fox Called Fauna

Written And Illustrated By

D S JOHNSON

ISBN 978-1-8380914-3-9

Copyright 2022 D S Johnson

J & J Publishing UK Croydon Surrey
E: JandJPublishingUK@yahoo.com

www.faunaandfriends.co.uk

Published in the United Kingdom

We don't own the earth; we belong to it, and we must share it with our wildlife. Steve Irwin

Once there was a fox named Fauna. She lived in a thicket, behind a row of houses on Croydon Lane. Fauna was a kind but shy fox who spent most of her time alone in her cosy den. She had a beautiful singing voice, and she loved to sing at night as she gathered food, collecting berries, insects and other tasty delights. Fauna lived happily on her own, but she felt lonely sometimes and wished she had friends to explore and have fun with.

One night, Fauna went exploring. She wanted to see the town beyond the thicket, so she made her way through the woods, towards the main road. A thick hedge marked the boundary of the woods and the town. As she got closer to the hedge, Fauna listened for cars and trucks. She had to be very careful

because it was very dangerous for her to cross a road. She listened carefully for noises, but it was quiet, so it was safe to keep moving. As she crawled through the hedge, Fauna used her nose to check for danger.
ONE SNIFF, TWO SNIFFS, look left, then look right.

Phew! It was all clear. She put her paw through the prickly bushes and carefully stepped out onto the pavement.

The street was very quiet, and the streetlights looked like giant fireflies. Fauna walked along the road looking at all the gardens and houses. At the front of each house was a shiny tower that sparkled in the night light.

As she walked, she caught a scent. She sniffed the air to find out where it was coming from. She went up close to one of the towers and put her little nose against it.

ONE SNIFF, TWO SNIFFS.

"What is that smell coming from inside?" she thought.

She sniffed it again, but she still couldn't tell what it was.

"There might be food in there," she thought. "Well, there's only one way to find out!"

Fauna pushed against the tower, but it didn't open.

"Maybe if I was a little taller, I could get it open," she

thought to herself. ONE, TWO, THREE, UP! She stood on her hind legs and tried again, but the lid still wouldn't budge. She walked around the tower to see if there was something else keeping it locked, but there wasn't, so she tried again. Once more, Fauna leapt onto her hind legs.

ONE, TWO, THREE, UP!
This time her paws reached the lid, but she leaned too far and lost her balance.
"Whoa!" she shouted.
Then, CRASH! The shiny tower toppled over, and

everything   fell out into the street.

"Oops!" said Fauna. "Oh dear, what a mess!"

Fauna looked around to see if anyone heard the noise, but the street was still quiet. She walked around the mess of food and rubbish.

"I wonder what this is," she thought.

ONE SNIFF, TWO SNIFFS, and a third SNIFF, just to be sure. Then Fauna smiled.

"Food!" she said excitedly. "Berries, my favourite! Oh, I do love fruit."

There was an assortment of fruit and vegetable scraps, berries, and some odd new fruit she had never eaten before. Fauna's new-found treats were delicious.

"Mmm!" she said with delight. "This is very tasty. I wish I could take some of this food home."

She looked through the scraps to see what she could take with her. Fauna was happy; the joy of finding all this lovely food bubbled up inside her and she began to sing. She sang and sang with all her might. "What lovely food on a lovely night!

Suddenly, there was a loud noise and her pointy ears pricked up. She looked up and down the street to see where the noise was coming from. Then she heard a loud shout.

"Shoo! Go Away! Stop that racket!"

Fauna was startled, but she stood still for a moment as she tried to understand why the angry man was shouting. She had no idea that her singing did not sound the same to humans as it does to animals, and she was very frightened. There was another loud noise, and the man came running down the street towards her and chased her away.
More lights turned on and it became very bright. Some of the other neighbours opened their windows and yelled at her to go away. Fauna ran back to the

thicket as fast as she could, down the road, through the hedge and into the woods. She looked back to make sure she wasn't followed, and then slowly walked to her den.

Henny Hedgehog and Bella Badger were walking together near the thicket. They were exploring the other side of the wood, near to Fauna's home. As they walked by a giant tree, they heard crying and went to see who it was. They found Fauna curled up and sobbing.

"Why are you crying?" asked Henny.

With a sob and a sigh, Fauna told them the whole story. Bella and Henny listened as Fauna told them everything, and they felt sad for her.

"There, there," said Bella as she tried to console her.

"That's terrible," said Henny. "You could have been hurt. You must be very careful when you go out alone." Then he smiled and stretched out his paw. "By the way, I'm Henny, and this is Bella."
Fauna lifted her tear-filled eyes and replied,
"I'm Fauna, pleased to meet you."
Then she rested her head on the soft moss.
"I'm very pleased to meet you too," said Bella.
"I'm so sorry this happened to you."

Fauna wiped her tears.

"I was so frightened," she said. "I think it was my singing that made him shout. When I'm happy, I sing loudly. I can't help it, but now I know my singing makes the people angry."

Fauna cradled her wet face in her tail.

"No, you must not think that," said Bella, "that was just a mean man."

"You know," said Henny, "we haven't heard you sing. Will you sing for us?"

"Yes, sing for us," Bella added. Fauna looked up at Henny and Bella.

"I've never sung for anyone before," said Fauna. "What if you don't like it. I wouldn't want you to be angry with me too." Bella shook her head.

"No," she said, "we would love to hear you sing."

"I bet your singing is fantastic!" said Henny excitedly. Fauna smiled and wiped her tears away. "You are both so kind, I'm very glad to have met you."

Then she stood up and took a deep breath, lifted her nose towards the starlit sky and began to sing. Bella and Henny smiled. They thought Fauna's singing was wonderful. The night wind carried Fauna's voice through the wood, and the other animals came out

to investigate the sweet sound. They gathered around her to listen to the beautiful song, and when she finished singing, all the animals clapped and cheered.

"You have a beautiful voice," said Bella. "Wow, that was amazing," said Henny.

Fauna was so happy she could burst.

"Thank you," she said with a smile. "I'm so glad my singing made you happy, thank you all."

Then, she walked over to Bella and Henny, touched her head with theirs and said, "Thank you for believing in me."

That night the animals had a party and got to know each other. They all brought food and they shared a meal together.

"Look!" said Bella as she pointed to the other animals laughing and having fun. "Your singing brought us all together."

Fauna looked around at everyone she lived with, but

never knew.

"It's amazing," she said.

"What's amazing?" asked Henny. Fauna replied,
"It's amazing how one song has given me so many
friends."

THE END

FUN FAUNA FACTS

Foxes are members of the dog family, and a female fox is called a Vixen.

Badgers are in the same family species as Otters and Weasels.

Foxes talk to each other with barks and screams. If you have heard a fox scream at night, it can sound scary, but they are just talking.

Badgers have strong limbs and claws which makes them excellent diggers.

Foxes are carnivores, and eat fruits and vegetables as well as wild birds, insects, and food they find in our bins.

The Word ·Badger ·comes from a French word meaning 'digger'.

The name Hedgehog is made up of two words. 'Hedge' because they build their home hedges and bushes and 'hog' because of the snorting sound they make.

Foxes will not hurt people unless they are provoked and they can live anywhere, either in towns or in the countryside

About The Author

D S Johnson is based in Surrey, England and is fond of nature and animals. History and the local surroundings hold much inspiration.

Other Titles in The Series

A Fox Called Fauna
A Hedgehog Called Henny
A Badger Called Bella

Books With Reader-Friendly Text and Language for All Abilities.

Created by D S Johnson Copyright 2009-2022